Cecil's New Adirondack Adventure

An adventure for kids in the Adirondack outdoors

Sheri Amsel

*For Quinn —
Have fun!
Sheri Amsel*

Adirondack Illustrator
P.O. Box 84
Elizabethtown, NY 12932
(518) 962-4977

amsels@westelcom.com
www.adirondackillustrator.com

In loving memory of my father,
Dr. Melvyn B. Amsel

Hello there, mouse fans...Cecil here, I am ready for another Adirondack adventure. Are *you*? Do you have your pencil? Do you have your eraser? Do you have your boots and insect repellent? We have fish to catch, hills to sled, mountains to hike and bugs to hunt. I'm getting tired just thinking about it. So...here we go!

antlers

osprey

goldenrod

aspen

hornet nest

red fox

zebra swallowtail

merganser

oak

gray squirrel

hawk

chickadee

caterpillar

coyote tracks

owl

red pine

raccoon

eagle

toad

mouse

moose

beaver

4

Circle the names of these Adirondack wild things...

H	N	L	D	V	K	H	L	I	B	H	Q	L	B	I	H	M	Q	Z	T
O	O	S	P	R	E	Y	A	X	A	N	T	L	E	R	S	B	H	E	D
P	Q	G	G	I	H	T	D	L	S	K	M	N	A	G	F	E	W	B	L
M	H	N	B	V	C	R	E	D	P	I	N	E	V	B	J	K	L	R	A
E	F	R	G	H	J	K	U	Y	E	R	E	W	E	A	G	L	E	A	N
R	B	G	H	O	R	N	E	T	N	E	S	T	R	A	S	D	F	S	X
G	R	A	Y	S	Q	U	I	R	R	E	L	G	D	E	R	T	O	W	L
A	A	F	R	G	H	H	K	E	R	T	Y	O	I	O	P	F	D	A	A
N	C	F	R	G	C	A	T	E	R	P	I	L	L	A	R	V	F	L	B
S	C	B	G	C	W	W	D	F	R	T	Y	D	K	L	M	M	P	L	Y
E	O	C	H	I	C	K	A	D	E	E	E	E	B	K	O	M	O	O	S
R	O	A	K	N	B	V	C	X	D	B	H	N	I	U	Y	T	R	W	T
M	N	N	H	T	R	D	S	C	F	E	R	R	B	V	G	F	R	T	B
V	V	P	C	G	H	J	I	K	O	P	M	O	U	S	E	T	O	A	D
T	V	H	H	U	Y	N	O	I	X	N	U	D	R	M	J	K	F	I	Z
V	G	F	S	A	E	M	I	U	Q	V	B	N	Y	U	I	O	P	L	Y
M	O	O	S	E	V	C	O	Y	O	T	E	T	R	A	C	K	S	T	I

Unscramble these common Adirondack creature's names.

L Q S R I R E U

squirrel

S W A R P O R

sparrow

E Y U K T R

Turkey

S E K A N

snake

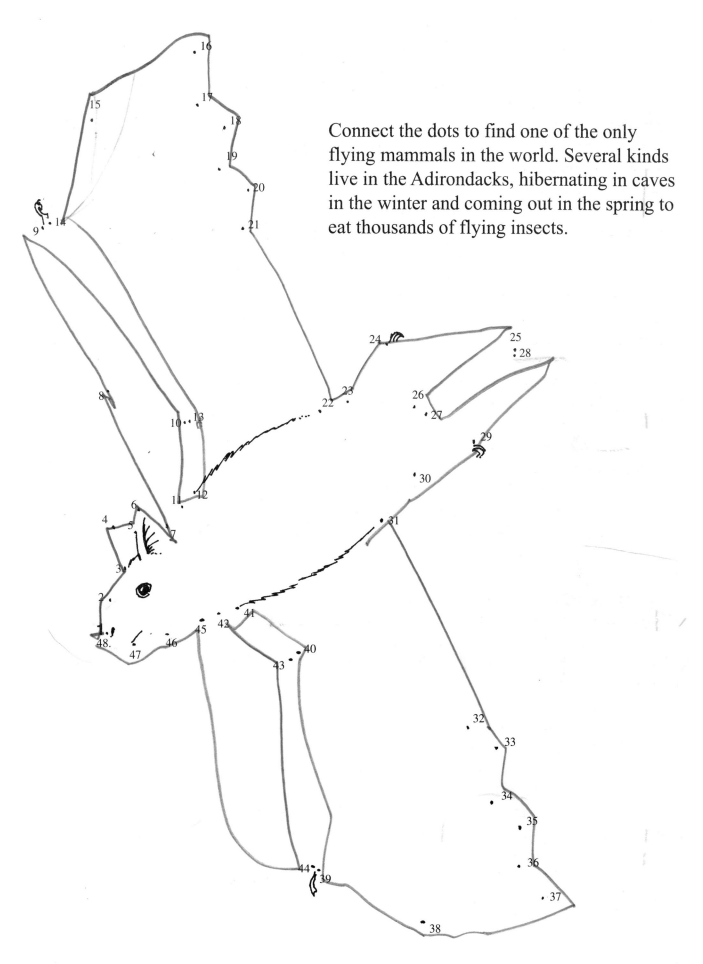

Connect the dots to find one of the only
flying mammals in the world. Several kinds
live in the Adirondacks, hibernating in caves
in the winter and coming out in the spring to
eat thousands of flying insects.

Fill in the crossword puzzle about the plants, animals and places of the Adirondacks.

ACROSS

1. Insect that begins as a caterpillar and ends up with brightly colored wings.
4. Large shade tree that had almost disappeared because of a disease carried from Holland by beetles.
5. Wildflower with yellow center and white petals.
6. Small blue dragonfly that lives near the water.
9. Tallest mountain in New York.
10. Capital of New York
11. Moisture that forms on cool nights on the grass and flowers.
12. Town near Whiteface mountain where Adirondack Life Magazine is made.
13. Large rodent that builds a lodge & came back from near extinction in 1847 from over-fur-trapping.
15. Buzzing insect that pollinates flowers.
16. Large black and white water bird with haunting call and red eyes.
17. Large bird of prey with white tail and head feathers.
20. Tree that makes acorns.
21. Tall water plants with cigar-shaped head found on ponds and marshes.
23. Fast flying insect with shiny, narrow wings that flies over ponds and wetlands chasing mosquitos.
25. Black and white mammal that sprays a smelly, toxic odor when startled.
26. Hornlike structures that grow on moose and deer for the fall.
27. Holds the seeds of pine trees.
29. Small seed-collecting rodent with stripe across eye and down side.
30. Very large, graceful, white bird with long neck that lives on ponds and lakes.
31. Largest canine, now very rare in the Adirondacks.
32. Fungus that grows on the forest floor with a stem and cap.

DOWN

1. A fish that comes in small mouth and large mouth.
2. Amphibian that lives on land, lays eggs in water and has bumpy, "warty" skin.
3. Yellow and black stinging insect that lives in the ground.
5. Barrier of sticks and branched made by beaver to block river flow.
7. Small rodent with a long tail.
8. Small red beetle with black spots.
14. Small mouse-sized rodent with short tail.
16. Large body of water where people fish, boat and swim.
18. Rare wildflower found in the woods in spring with unusual pink bloom shaped like hollow ball.
19. Second tallest mountain in New York.
20. The worldwide sporting event held in Lake Placid in 1932 and 1980.
22. Wild canines with bushy tails.
23. Male duck.
24. Small insect that travels in groups and is famous for ruining picnics!
28. Small amphibian, often orange-red with spots.

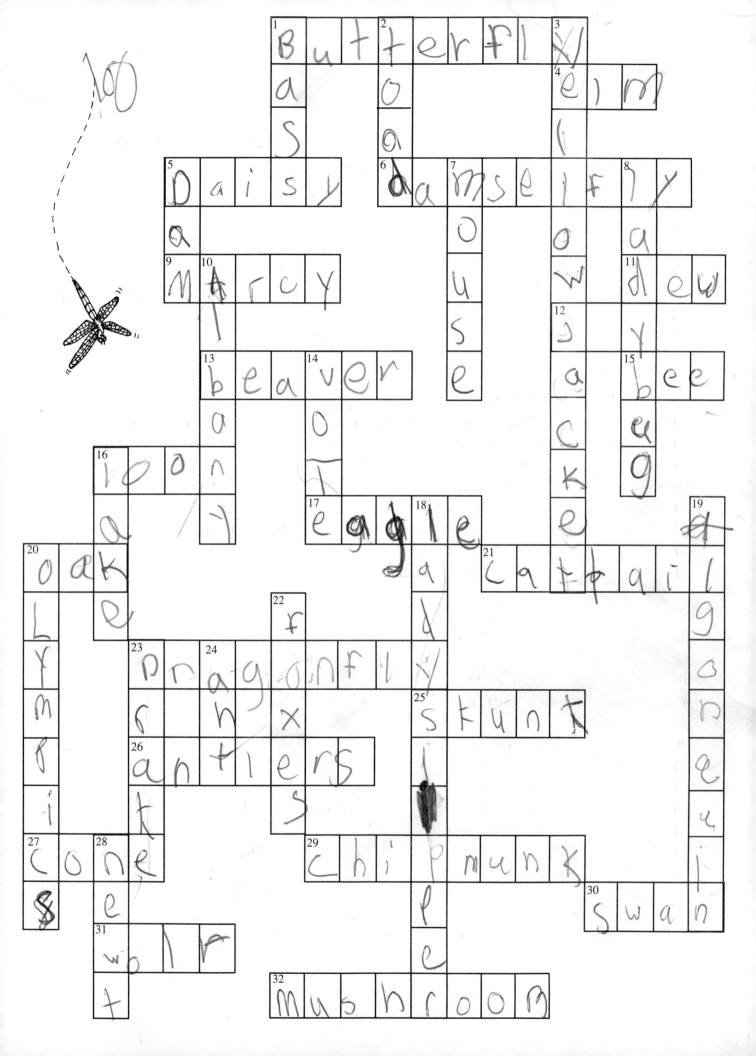

Connect the Adirondack animals to the foods they like to eat...

Out on a toboggan ride, Cecil has lost his way. Help him find the right trail back to the bonfire to warm his cold toes.

Cecil loves to fish! Help him name the fish he is catching
by drawing a line from the name tag to the fish.

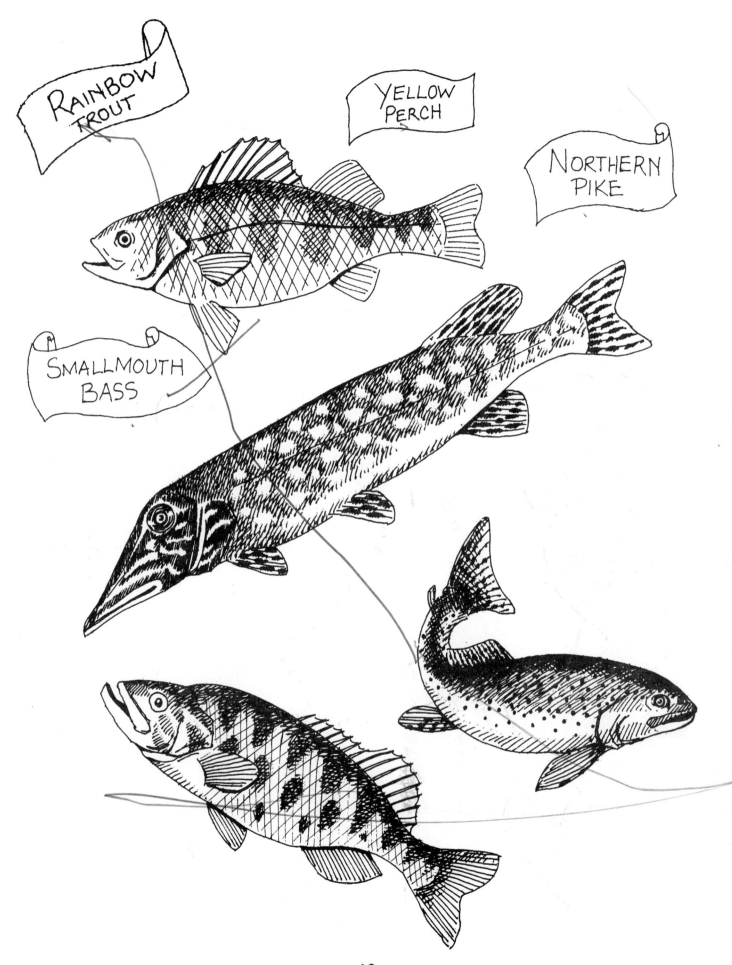

RAINBOW TROUT

YELLOW PERCH

NORTHERN PIKE

SMALLMOUTH BASS

Connect the dots to find the largest rodent in North America. Trapped for it's fur until it was almost extinct in the 1800's, now this hard-working mammal is found all over the Adirondacks wherever there is running water and trees.

Cutting his Christmas tree in the woods, Cecil got caught out after dark. Help him find his way back to his warm house, so he can set up his tree!

Learn to draw with Cecil.
Follow the steps one by one and draw the Adirondack bugs.

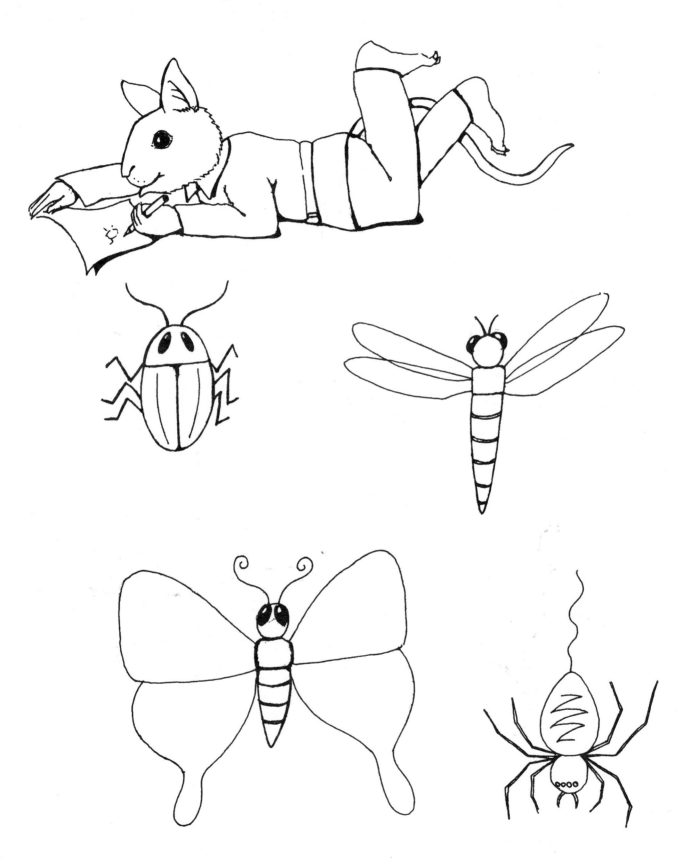

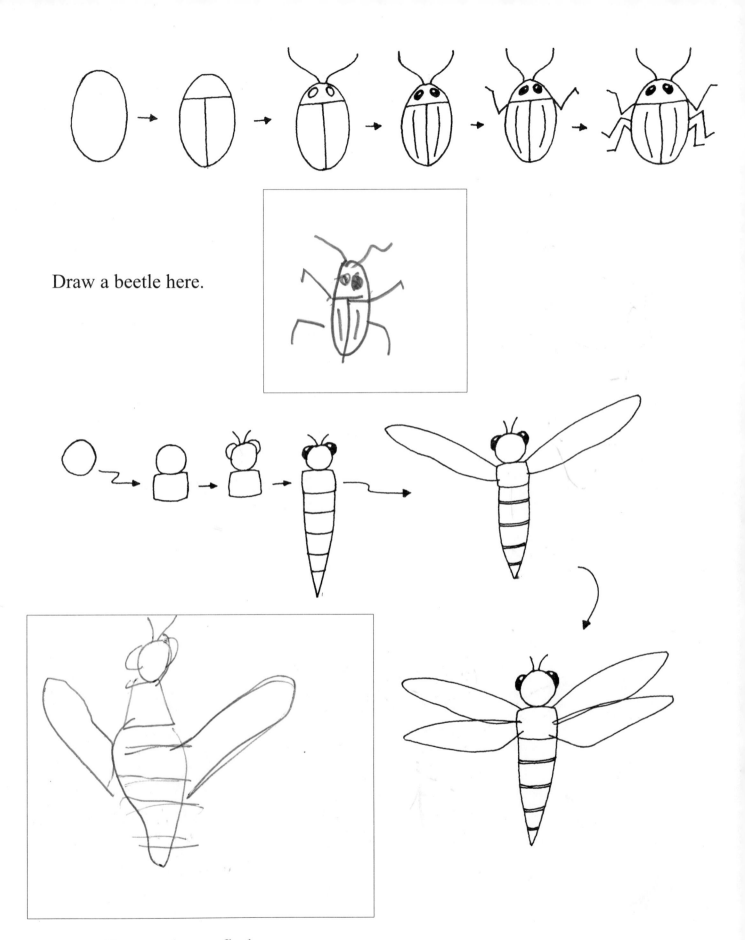

Draw a beetle here.

Draw a dragonfly here.

More drawing on the next page...

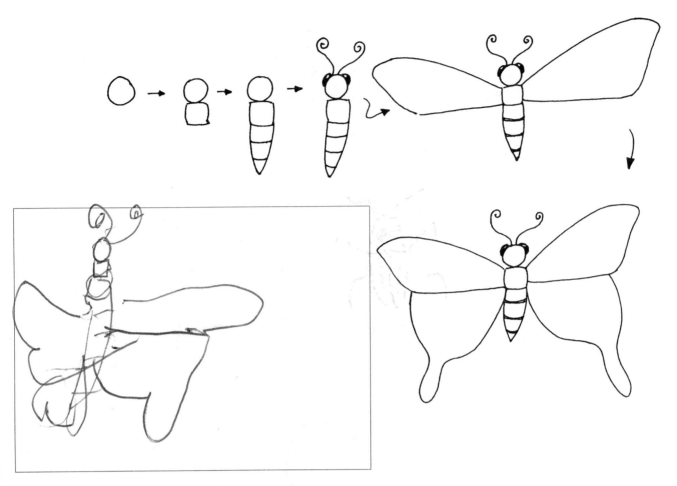

Draw a butterfly here.

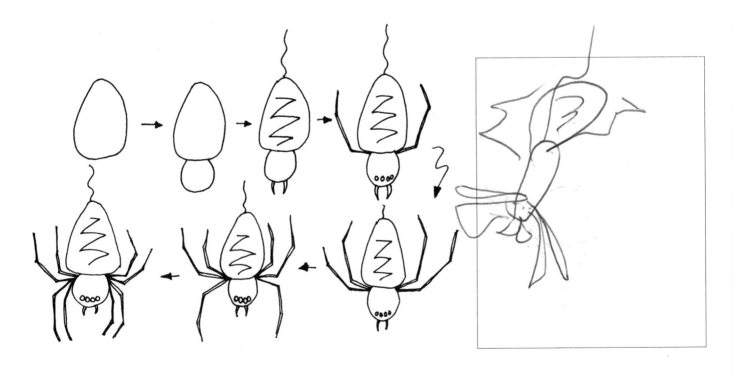

Draw a spider here.

Help Cecil find 25 dragonflies.

Connect the dots to find the tallest bird in the Adirondacks. Eating fish and other small animals, this bird is found near water and will stay up north until the ponds and lakes freeze in late fall.

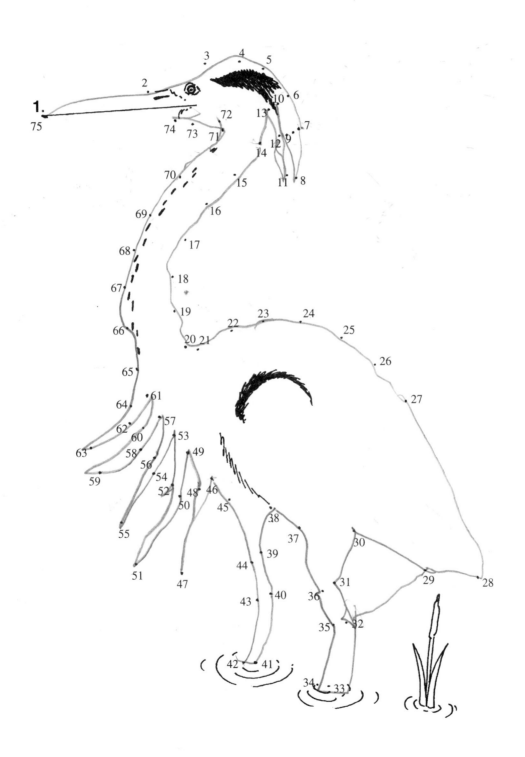

Cecil loves to identify insects. Help him catch the butterfly so he can name it and release it before dark.

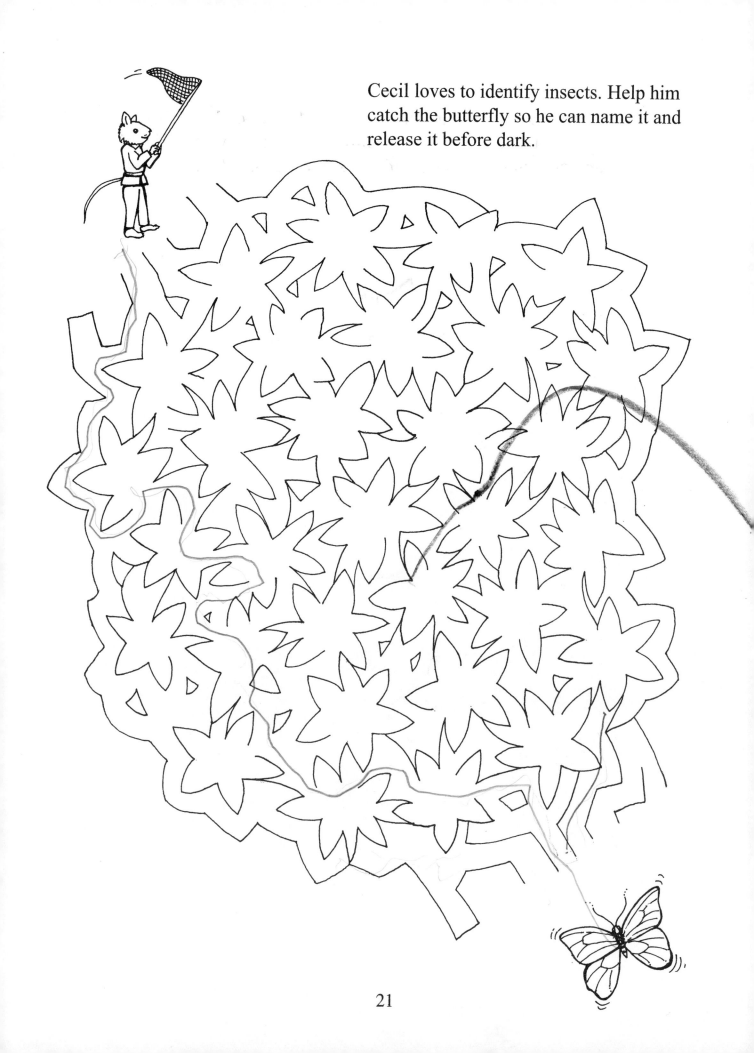

Sitting by a pond Cecil noticed lots of insects and spiders doing their work. Help him find five mayflies, five mosquitos and five spiders hidden in the wetland plants.

22

23

Cecil is learning the names of the trees.
He labeled each one but the wind blew the labels away.
Help him connect the label with the right tree.

Connect the dots to find one of the birds that
spends the whole winter in the Adirondacks.

10

11 12

13. 14 15 16

2   3

1.
42

4
5

6

7

41

9

40

8

39

26

25

17

38

27

37

28

36

32 30
34   29
31
35 33

24

18

20
19
22
21

23

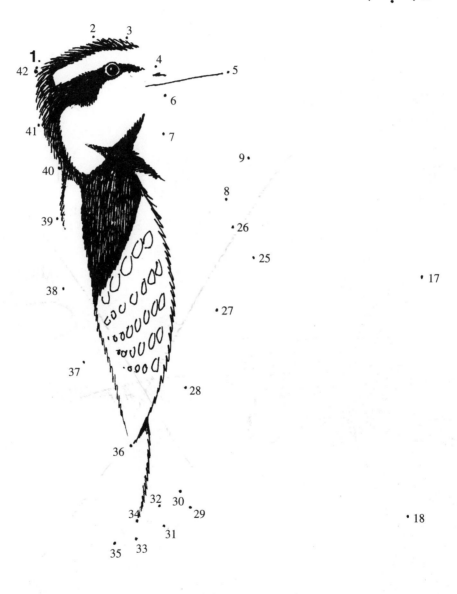

Connect the Adirondack animals with their tracks.

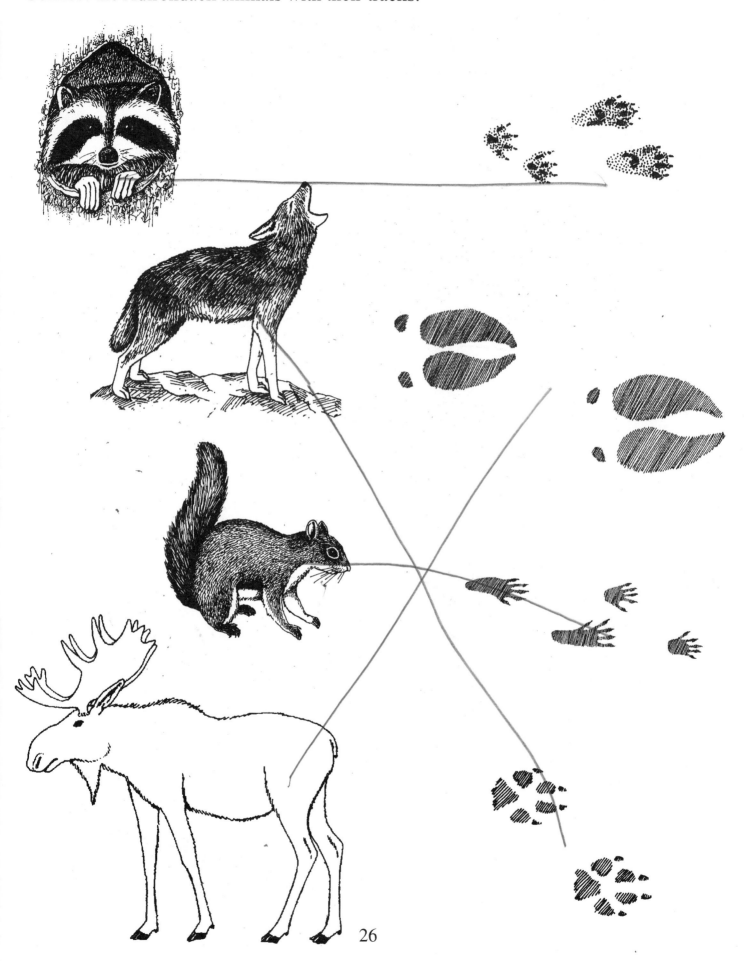

Cecil took too long cutting sticks in the woods for roasting marshmallows. Help him hurry home before the fire dies out.

Solutions...

Page 4 - word search:

Page 6 - word scramble
Squirrel
Sparrow
Turkey
Snake

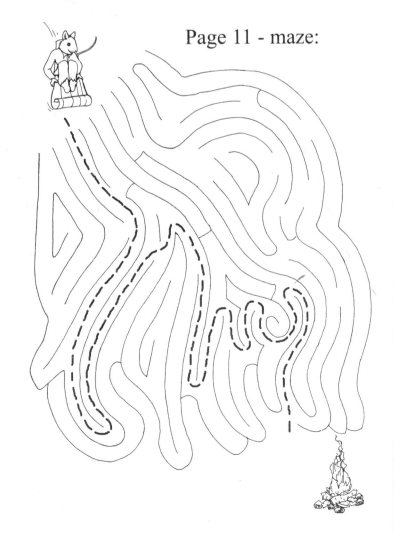

Word search grid:

H	N	L	D	V	K	H	L	I	B	H	Q	L	B	I	H	M	Q	Z	T
O	O	S	P	R	E	Y	A	X	A	N	T	L	E	R	S	B	H	E	D
P	Q	G	G	I	H	T	D	L	S	K	M	N	A	G	F	E	W	B	L
M	H	N	B	V	C	R	E	D	P	I	N	E	V	B	J	K	L	R	A
E	F	R	G	H	J	K	U	Y	E	R	E	W	E	A	G	L	E	A	N
R	B	G	H	O	R	N	E	T	N	E	S	T	R	A	S	D	F	S	X
G	R	A	Y	S	Q	U	I	R	R	E	L	G	D	E	R	T	O	W	L
A	A	F	R	G	H	H	K	E	R	T	Y	O	I	O	P	F	D	A	A
N	C	F	R	G	C	A	T	E	R	P	I	L	L	A	R	V	F	L	B
S	C	B	G	C	W	W	D	F	R	T	Y	D	K	L	M	M	P	L	Y
E	O	C	H	I	C	K	A	D	E	E	E	E	B	K	O	M	O	O	S
R	O	A	K	N	B	V	C	X	D	B	H	N	I	U	Y	T	R	W	T
M	N	N	H	T	R	D	S	C	F	E	R	R	B	V	G	F	R	T	B
V	V	P	C	G	H	J	I	K	O	P	M	O	U	S	E	T	O	A	D
T	V	H	H	U	Y	N	O	I	X	N	U	D	R	M	J	K	F	I	Z
V	G	F	S	A	E	M	I	U	Q	V	B	N	Y	U	I	O	P	L	Y
M	O	O	S	E	V	C	O	Y	O	T	E	T	R	A	C	K	S	T	I

Page 8 - crossword puzzle:

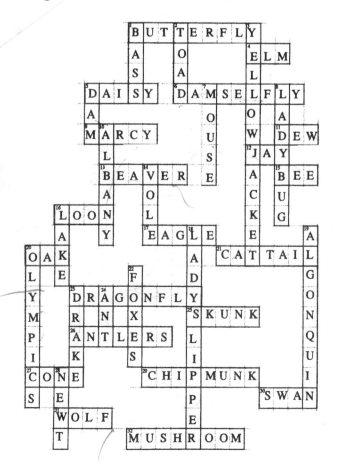

Page 11 - maze:

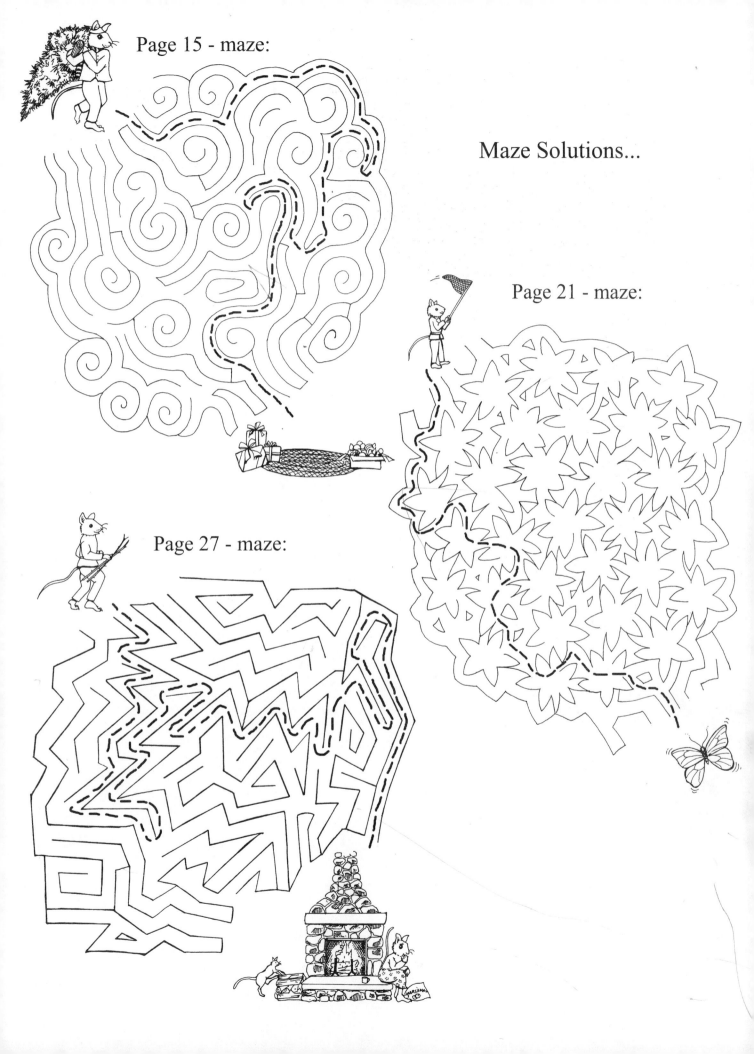

Page 15 - maze:

Maze Solutions...

Page 21 - maze:

Page 27 - maze:

Page 19 -
hidden dragonflies:

Page 23 - hidden bugs:

Page 24 - tree ID:

WHITE PINE

MAPLE

HEMLOCK

BEECH

OAK

Page 26 - animal tracks:

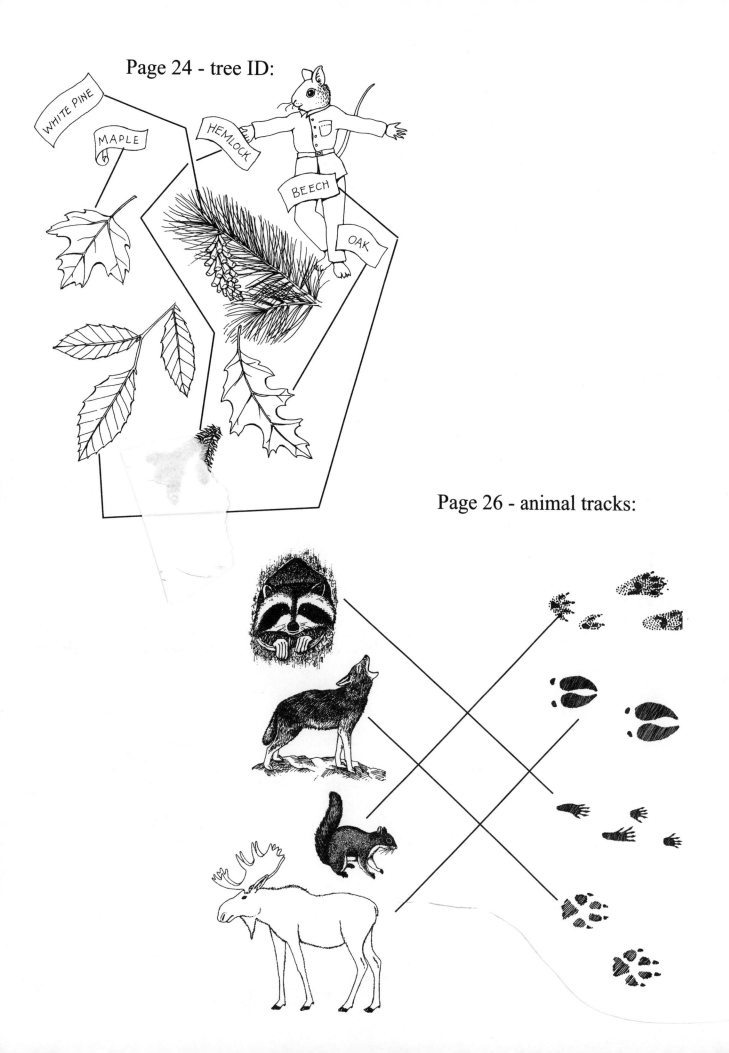

Thanks for going on my adventure! If you are interested in more Adirondack books and stuff by my friend Sheri Amsel you can go to:
www.adirondackillustrator.com

AND....as a special gift, cut out this coupon and get free shipping when you order any Adirondack T-shirts or books from the website.

For all Cecil lovers...
Free shipping on any product ordered from:

www.adirondackillustrator.com

Teachers! I have special pull with the publisher....so if you would like to photocopy any of the Adirondack activities in this book for classroom use only, email for the quickest and easiest permission:
amsels@westelcom.com
Good luck with all your adventures,
Cecil A. Mouse